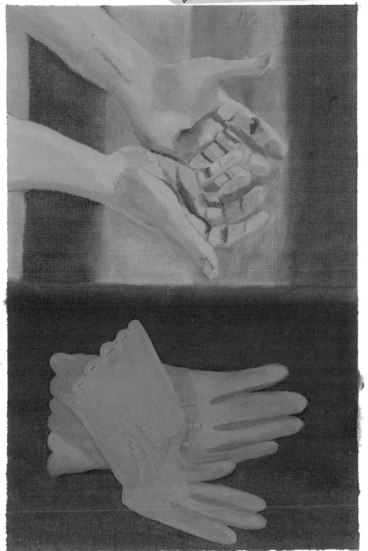

HIGH AND DRY

Also by Richard Russo

RICHARD RUSSO

High and Dry

Down East
MAINE

Copyright © 2012 by Richard Russo
All rights reserved

Cover and insert art © Kate Russo

"High and Dry" originally appeared in *Granta*

Designed by Miroslaw Jurek

ISBN 978-1-60893-185-9

Printed in the United States on papers from sustainably harvested forests

Library of Congress Cataloging-in-Publication data:
Russo, Richard, 1949-
  Interventions : a novella & three stories / by Richard Russo ; artwork by Kate Russo.
    p. cm.
  ISBN 978-1-60893-185-9 (pbk. in slipcase : alk. paper)
  I. Russo, Kate, 1982- II. Title.
  PS3568.U812I58 2012
  813'.54--dc23
                          2012000434

Down East
Books · Magazine · Online
downeast.com
Distributed to the trade by National Book Network

A few years ago a friend of mine, passing the sign on the New York State Thruway for THE CENTRAL LEATHERSTOCKING REGION, misread the word *leatherstocking* for *laughingstock*, and thought, "That must be where Russo's from." She was right. I'm from Gloversville, just a few miles north in the foothills of the Adirondacks, a place that's easy to joke about unless you live there, as some of my family still do.

In its heyday nine out of ten dress gloves manufactured in the United States came from Gloversville. By the end of the nineteenth century craftsmen from all over Europe had flocked in, and for decades the gloves produced there were on a par with the finest made anywhere in the world. Back then glove cutting was governed by a guild. You apprenticed, as my maternal grandfather did, typically for two or three years. The primary tools of a guild-trained glovecutter's trade were his eye, his experience of animal skins, and his imagination. It was my grandfather who gave me my very first lessons in art — though

I doubt he would've put it like that — when he explained the challenge of making something truly fine and beautiful from an imperfect animal hide. After they're tanned but before they go to the cutter, skins are rolled and brushed and finished to ensure smooth uniformity, but inevitably they retain some of nature's flaws. The true craftsman, he gave me to understand, works around these flaws or figures out how to incorporate them into the glove's natural folds or stitching. Each skin posed a problem whose solution required imagination. The glove-cutter's job wasn't just to get as many gloves as possible out of a skin, but to do so while minimizing its flaws.

Leather had been tanned in Fulton County, using the bark from local hemlock trees, since before the American Revolution. Gloversville and neighboring Johnstown were home to all things leather — shoes and coats and handbags and furniture, not only gloves. My other grandfather, from Palermo, Italy, had heard about this place where so many leather artisans had gathered in upstate New York, and so he journeyed to America in hopes of making a living there as a shoemaker. From New York City he took the train north to Albany, then west as far as the Barge Canal hamlet of Fonda, where he followed the freight tracks north as far as Johnstown, where I was born years later. Did he have any real idea of where he was headed, or what his new life would be like? You tell me. Among the few material possessions he brought with him from the old country was an opera cape.

Both men had wretched timing. My Italian grandfather learned quickly that Fulton County wasn't New York City, and that few men in his new home would buy expensive custom-made shoes instead of comparatively inexpensive machine-made ones, so he had little choice but to become a shoe repairman. And by the time my maternal grandfather arrived in Gloversville from Vermont, the real craft of glove cutting was already under assault. By the end of World War I, many gloves were being "pattern cut." (For a size-six glove, a size-six pattern was affixed to the skin and cut around with shears.) Once he returned from World War II the process was largely mechanized by "clicker" cutting machines that quickly stamped out pre-sized gloves, requiring the operator only to position the tanned skin under the machine's lethal blades and pull down on its mechanical arm. I was born in 1949, and by then there wasn't much demand for expensive handmade gloves or shoes, but both my grandfathers had made their big moves to Fulton County and staked their dubious claims, so there they remained. It was also during the first half of the twentieth century that chrome tanning, a chemical process that made leather more supple and water resistant, and dramatically sped up the tanning process, became the industry standard, replacing traditional vegetable tanning and making tanneries even more hazardous, not just for the workers, but also for those who lived nearby and, especially, downstream. Speed, efficiency, and technology had trumped art and craft.

That said, between 1890 and 1950 people in Gloversville made money, some of them a lot of it. Drive along Kingsboro Avenue, which parallels Main Street, and have a gander at the fine old houses set back from the street and well apart from one another, and you'll get a sense of the prosperity that at least some enjoyed until World War II. Even downtown Gloversville, which by the 1970s had become a Dresden-like ruin, still shows signs of that old wealth. The Andrew Carnegie Gloversville Free Library is as lovely as can be, and the old high school, which sits atop a gentle hill, bespeaks a community that once believed in itself and that good times would not be fleeting. On its sloping lawn stands a statue of Nathan Littaur, one of the richest men in the county, whose extended arm appears to point at the grand marble edifice of the Eccentric Club, which refused him membership because he was a Jew. Down the street is the recently restored Glove Theater, where I spent just about every Saturday afternoon of my adolescence. There was also a charming old hotel, the Kingsboro, in whose elegant dining room Monsignor Kreugler, whom I'd served as an altar boy at Sacred Heart Church, held weekly court after his last Sunday Mass. Since it was razed, visitors to Gloversville have had to stay in nearby Johnstown, out on the arterial highway that was supposed to breathe new life into the town but instead, all too predictably, allowed people to race by, without stopping or even slowing down, en route to Saratoga, Lake George, or Montreal.

How quickly it all happened. In the fifties, on a Saturday afternoon, downtown Gloversville would be gridlocked with cars honking hellos at pedestrians. The sidewalks were so jammed with shoppers that, as a boy trapped among taller adults, I had to depend on my mother, herself no giant, to navigate us from one store to the next or, more harrowingly, across Main Street. Often, when we finished what we called our weekly "errands," my mother and I would stop in at Pedrick's. Located next to city hall, it was a dark, cool place, the only establishment of my youth that was air conditioned, a long, thin wall whose service window allowed sodas and cocktails to be passed from the often raucous bar into the more respectable restaurant. Back then Pedrick's was always mobbed, even in the middle of a Saturday afternoon. Mounted on the wall of each booth was a mini-jukebox whose moveable mechanical pages were full of song listings. Selections made here — five for a quarter, if memory serves — were played on the real jukebox on the far wall. We always played the jukebox, a whole quarter's worth, while nursing sodas served so cold they made my teeth hurt. Sometimes, though, the music was drowned out by rowdy male laughter from the bar, where the wall-mounted television was tuned to a Yankees ball game, and if anybody hit a home run everyone in the restaurant knew it immediately. I remember listening intently to all the men's voices, trying to pick out my father's. He and my mother had separated when I was little, but he was still around town and I always imagined him on the other side of that wall in Pedrick's.

I also suspected that my mother, if she hadn't been saddled with me, would have preferred to be over there. She liked men, liked being among them, and the restaurant side was mostly women and kids and older people. Though I couldn't have put it into words, I had the distinct impression that the wall separating respectability from fun was very thin indeed. There was another jukebox in the bar, and sometimes it got cranked up loud enough to compete with whatever was playing on ours, and then my mother would say it was time to go, as if she feared the wall itself might come crashing down. To her, music getting pumped up like that could only mean one thing: that people over there were dancing, middle of the afternoon or not, and if she'd been there, it would have been her as well. A good decade after the end of World War II, Gloversville was still in a party mode, and regular Saturday festivities routinely continued right up to last call and often beyond, the town's prosperous citizens dancing and drinking at the Eccentric Club, the more middle-class folk in the blue-collar taverns along upper Main Street or, in summer, at the pavilion at nearby Caroga Lake, the poor (often the most recent immigrants with the lowest paying tannery jobs) in the gin mills bordering South Main in the section of town referred to as the Gut, where arrests for drunkenness or indecency or belligerence were much more likely to be recorded in the local newspaper on Monday than comparable exploits at the Eccentric Club.

By the time I graduated from high school in 1967,

you could have strafed Main Street with automatic weapon fire without endangering a soul. On Saturday afternoons the sidewalks were deserted, people in newly reduced circumstances shopping for bargains at the cheap, off-brand stores that had sprung up along the arterial. Jobless men would emerge from the pool hall or one of the seedy gin mills that sold cheap draft beer and rot-gut rye, blinking into the afternoon light and flexing at the knees. Lighting up a smoke, they'd peer up Main Street in one direction, then down the other, as if wondering where the hell everybody went. By then the restaurant side of Pedrick's had closed, but since I turned eighteen that summer, now of legal drinking age, the other side was no longer off limits. Now, though, it was quiet as a library, the half dozen grizzled, solitary drinkers rotating on their stools when the door opened, as if out of the brightness the past might saunter in, trailing ten-dollar bills in its wake. Most of my friends were going to college close to home, at the Albany branch of the state university, or one of the small Catholic colleges, or the community college just down the road, whereas I was heading west to the University of Arizona in an old, dangerously underpowered Ford Galaxie and pulling a U-haul that contained all my mother's worldly goods. She'd found a job, she told me, in nearby Phoenix, and she meant to escape once and for all this self-satisfied Podunk town that everybody finally conceded had no future. Still, every now and then that summer of '67, I'd poke my head into Pedrick's to see if my father was among those drinking Utica Club drafts at the bar. But, like time itself, he, too, had moved on.

Globalism: A Primer

What happened? Lots of things. After World War II, about the same time men stopped wearing hats, women stopped wearing gloves. When Jackie Kennedy wore a pair at her husband's inauguration, the clock got turned back for a while, but the trend proved irreversible. More importantly, glove-making started going overseas where labor was cheap. Gloversville went bust the way Mike Campbell declares his bankruptcy in Hemingway's *The Sun Also Rises*, "gradually and suddenly." The "giant sucking sound" of globalism came to Gloversville decades early and with a vengeance. My maternal grandfather, who, despite being a veteran of two world wars, had been branded a communist from the pulpit of Sacred Heart Church for being a union man, saw it coming even before crappy Asian-made gloves showed up in the shops, where a few buttons could be sewn on and the gloves stamped "made in Gloversville." Around Thanksgiving, the off-season in the glove business, workers in the skin mills got laid off, and every year it took a little longer for them to be called back. Worse, they weren't all rehired at once, which practice allowed the shop owners to remind their employees that things were different now. What mattered was moving inventory down the line, not quality. After all, Asians and Indians were doing what Gloversville men did at a quarter of the cost.

My grandfather, who came home from the Pacific with malaria and soon afterward developed emphysema, was by then too sick to fight. He continued to work as always, refusing to cut corners and, as a result, making considerably less money than men who were willing to do things slapdash. The bosses could exploit him, give him the most flawed skins and treat him like a robot instead of the craftsman he was, but he claimed the one thing they couldn't order him to do was a bad job. But of course they didn't need to. You only had to look at how his narrow, concave chest heaved as he struggled to draw oxygen into his failing lungs to know he wouldn't be anybody's problem much longer. His wife, who'd survived the Depression, foresaw a diminished future. She began stocking the pantry with cans of wax beans and tuna fish earlier every year, aware that this time the layoffs would likely last longer, that her husband, who was growing sicker by the day, would be among the last called back. Jesus on his best day could do no more with loaves and fishes than my grandmother did with a pound of bacon. Still, it was just a matter of time.

Flight

So when I resolved to head out west to college, my mother decided to make it a jailbreak and come along, though for a long time she kept that plan to herself. You could hardly blame her for wanting out. By then she was divorced and still relatively young. We'd lived all those years in a well-maintained middle-class neighborhood, sharing a modest two-family house, her parents in the two-bedroom, single-bath downstairs flat, she and I in the identically configured one above. My grandfather, who'd never before purchased anything he couldn't pay for with cash out of his wallet, bought that house on Helwig Street, I suspect, because he knew my parents' marriage was on the rocks and that my mother and I would need a place to live. Though she never would have admitted it, even to herself, she must have felt at least a little guilty about leaving now, fifteen years later, especially given her father's poor health. You don't get better from emphysema; you get worse, and his working days by then were done. An oxygen tank sat behind his chair in the living room. On cold days he couldn't go outdoors without a cloth mask, and even the easy stroll down to the mailbox at the end of the block tuckered him out. My mother kept her secret as long as she could, but eventually had to come clean. Having subsidized us over the years in small and sometimes larger ways, my grandparents were of the opinion that she couldn't make it out west on her own (she didn't own a car or even know how to drive), which made her even more determined to prove them wrong. In the months before we departed, they argued nonstop, and by the time we packed the U-Haul with what little my mother hadn't sold, they were barely speaking. Though aware of the discord, I was spared its worst effects because from the time I was little they had agreed never to argue in front of me; so I don't know what specific charges were leveled, who accused whom of what, how specific my grandparents were about their daughter's long history of underestimating life's costs and difficulties. Oddly enough, my sense was that their ongoing argument centered on Gloversville.

Okay, maybe not the town itself. After all, my mother had grown up there and occasionally still harbored deep affection for it, an affection that would well up from some remote corner of her heart whenever she left. During her time in Phoenix she came to speak of Gloversville with something like longing, as if she'd been banished by cruel decree. Though I'd never encountered this before, the pattern was all too familiar to my grandparents. As a girl my mother couldn't wait to go away to college, but was terribly homesick when she got there and quit after a year, returning home to work as a telephone operator. Two short years later, when the army stationed my father in Georgia, she followed him there eagerly, like a bird released from a cage, but she didn't like the South and as soon as he shipped overseas she returned to Gloversville just as eagerly.

By the time I came along, Gloversville had come to represent to my mother everything that was keeping her from living the finer life to which she was intended. She thought of herself as modern and free-thinking, whereas her home town was backward and parochial. More than anything what she longed for, first as a girl and later as a woman, was independence from scrutiny and interference, and the freedom to exercise her own judgment, which she believed to be excellent. All Gloversville offered was structure: church, neighbors, work, Sunday picnics with family at the lake — with her parents, right downstairs, second-guessing her every decision. If she stayed put, my grandparents argued, she'd be safe. But she didn't want to be safe. She wanted to be free.

Had I been asked my opinion, I might have weighed in, but probably not. As a high-school senior I was by definition already gone, as anxious as any other seventeen-year-old to embrace whatever came next. Like most of my friends, I knew that wouldn't be in Gloversville. For decades the mill owners had in effect run the town, and even as the leather industry slipped deeper into decline it kept other industries out, or so it was widely believed. If you were young, the conventional wisdom held that you had to go away and make something of yourself elsewhere — as a doctor or lawyer or pharmacist — before it made sense to return. My grandparents, unlike my mother, didn't hate Gloversville, but they understood the skin mills were finished, and anyway mill life was a drudgery they wouldn't have wished on me even if it were lucrative. My grandfather, too young for the First World War and too old for the

Second, had nevertheless served in both, and as a boy I assumed this because he was very brave, very patriotic. Which he was, but war also offered him a respite from the shops. His wife, thinking of him on a ship in the South Pacific during World War II, was envious, if you can believe it, of the great adventure he was on, while she was left behind to measure out the long, gray days with their two daughters as best she could in a town she'd never wanted to move to anyway, because it took her away from her sisters. But neither she nor my grandfather blamed Gloversville for their circumscribed lives. They didn't spend a lot of time worrying about whether it was better or worse than other places. It was simply where they were, where they would remain.

And my own feelings about Gloversville? As a boy I'd been happy as a clam there. Our block on Helwig Street was neighborly, with a grocery store situated diagonally across the street. My mother's sister and her family lived around the corner on Sixth Avenue, which meant I grew up surrounded by cousins. In kindergarten and first grade, my grandmother walked me to school in the morning and was there to meet me in the afternoon, and in the summers we went for walks to a lovely little park a few blocks away. On weekends it was often my grandfather who'd take my hand and together we'd head downtown for a bag of "peatles," his peculiar word for red-skinned peanuts, stopping on the way back to visit with neighbors on their porches. By the time I was old enough to get my first bike and explore beyond Helwig Street, I'd discovered the magic of baseball and so, wooden bat over my shoulder, mitt dangling from my handlebars, I disappeared with friends for whole mornings or afternoons or both. At my aunt's there was a basketball hoop up over the garage, and during the long winters my cousin Greg and I kept the driveway shoveled meticulously so we could shoot baskets, even when it was so cold the net froze and you couldn't dribble the ball. Come autumn I raked leaves, stealing this job from my grandfather, who loved to do it, though he didn't always have sufficient breath. Sometimes he'd start the job and I finished while he snuck a cigarette around back of the house where my grandmother couldn't see him. Summers I mowed lawns, and winters I shoveled sidewalks, jobs I continued straight through high school, even though by then I had other part-time, after-school employment. I fell in love with one local girl after another. Was something missing? Anything amiss?

Yet when the time came I fled. I didn't *leave*, as everyone else my age was doing. I fled, fled as if I'd committed a crime and the authorities were closing in, the window of escape closing fast. As if I feared or even loathed the place I knew and the people I loved.

The Foothills

One winter, when I was ten or eleven and had expressed some fondness for or appreciation of our lives, my mother's face clouded over and she announced, "*You* are going to see something of the world outside Gloversville."

Vacation, she meant, and that summer we went, just the two of us, to Martha's Vineyard. The island wasn't nearly so famous then, and I don't know where she got the idea. Probably somebody from General Electric had gone there. Much of what my mother knew about the world outside of Gloversville derived from her eight-to-five weekday life in the Computer Room in Schenectady, loading and unloading large wheel-like tape drives onto a computer the size of a bus. It was probably less powerful than today's low-end laptops, but engineers and programmers came from all over the U.S. and even Europe to crunch their numbers, and my mother trusted these men as much as any newsreel or oracle. At any rate, one deep winter day a manila envelope chock full brochures for posh hotels and graceful inns arrived from the island's chamber of commerce. My mother pored over them as if she feared there'd be a quiz when we stepped off the ferry. The resort she settled on was near Menemsha, on the more remote and sparsely populated side of the island. The main inn was large and rambling, with a huge porch and an elegant dining room with a westward view of the sound, the better to view the magnificent sunsets. Between the inn and the water was a large sloping lawn dotted with tiny cottages, and it was one of these that we rented. Instead of being cheek by jowl with other vacationers, my mother reasoned, *we'd* have privacy *and* be closer to the water, though even a ten-year-old boy could plainly see that the cottages were cheaper. The attraction of this particular resort was that it operated on the American plan, which meant that three meals were included; she could pay up front with no fear of surprise charges. She called twice that spring after we'd booked our stay, just to make sure she hadn't misunderstood that part.

Perhaps because my mother was so focused on how much it was going to cost, she didn't tumble to the fact that it was a Jewish resort, probably the only one on the island. Still, if her goal was to introduce me to something of the wider world, she'd chosen the right spot. Among our fellow vacationers were a dancer and a pianist and a playwright. Perhaps because of how out of place we appeared, we were immediately befriended. A young college student gave me tennis lessons when I showed up at the courts, no doubt looking forlorn, just as he and his girlfriend were finishing a match. When it rained one day, another couple took us into Oak Bluffs to see the gingerbread cottages. A woman roughly my mother's age and also separated from her husband sometimes came with us to the beach. She wore a startlingly brief swimsuit, which caused me to fall in love with her, and I remember being devastated when, instead of joining us in the dining room, she went out on dinner dates to Edgartown and Vineyard Haven. Judging by the number of men who stopped by our table to introduce themselves, my mother, but for me, would have done the same.

Lest I miss the significance of all we observed that week, my mother provided a running commentary, as if she didn't trust me to arrive at valid conclusions. Notice, she said, how these people had manners, how they didn't dress or talk or shamble around like Gloversville folk. They were educated, as one day I would be, and to them home was New York or

Boston, which somehow meant that they could stay for all of July, maybe even the whole summer, whereas because of *our* home, we had to scrimp and save for just one week. Notice, she said, how when people asked us where we were from and I said Gloversville, we then had to explain where it was, which meant our town wasn't the center of anyone's universe but our own. "But the Adirondacks are so beautiful," people objected, anxious to concede that we lived someplace nice. "The *foothills* of the Adirondacks," my mother clarified, giving me to understand that we, neither up nor down, had cleverly contrived to have the worst of both worlds.

It was an expensive week in more ways than one. My mother had financed the trip by brown-bagging an entire year's worth of cheese sandwiches instead of going out for lunch with her coworkers, and we'd blown the whole wad in seven short days, after which there was nothing to do but return to our foothills. The island ferry dropped us in Woods Hole, where we waited for a bus to take us to Providence, then for another to Albany, and finally for the one to the Four Corners in Gloversville. By the time we arrived we were so tapped out that my mother had to borrow money from my grandparents until she could collect her next paycheck at GE. Even more discouraging, from her perspective, was that nobody wanted to hear about the marvelous island we'd visited, the classy people we'd met, the exciting things we'd done. No one expressed the slightest desire to duplicate our experience the following summer, though my mother was anxious to share the brochures she'd saved, the ferry schedule, the postcards she purchased as mementos. I managed to make matters worse, as I usually did back then, by telling her how glad I was to be home. What I meant, of course, was that I'd missed my grandparents and my cousins and not one but two American Legion baseball games. What she heard, though, was that I preferred the place she loathed. For a whole year she'd sacrificed to show me something better, and I had failed to appreciate it.

Alright, then, she decided, no more *showing*. From then on she meant to lay down the law. "You're *going* to college," she informed me, as if by saying I was glad to be home, I'd called into question that long-range goal. "You're getting *out* of this place. Do you understand?" When I said I did, she asked me the same question again, and only when I gave the same answer did she go to the store and buy more sliced American cheese and rye bread. These future savings would now go into my college fund. By the time we left for Arizona they amounted to a little over four thousand dollars. Not much, unless you think of it as eight years' worth of cheese sandwiches in 1960s dollars.

But if she thought I wasn't paying attention on Martha's Vineyard, she was wrong. I'd been as enchanted as she was by the island and everyone we'd met there. I'd loved the crashing waves and clam chowder and tennis so much that I returned home feeling ashamed of where we lived, of our neighbors whose leaves I raked and snow I shoveled and lawns I mowed, and of how people farther down Helwig Street sat shirtless on their sloping porches in warm weather, scratching their bellies and leaning forward when a car they didn't recognize rounded the corner, wondering out loud who *that* was and where they were headed. After Martha's Vineyard I noticed things about our family, too, the way we talked over one another at holiday gatherings, our voices rising, screeching *No, no, you're telling it wrong*, because of course these stories belonged to all of us and we knew their details by heart. Martha's Vineyard people didn't interrupt; before entering the conversation they waited politely until whoever was speaking had finished. "There's no reason to raise your voice here," my mother had to keep reminding me. When we saw people in the dining room we'd met the day before, everybody stood up and we all shook hands. "Did you notice how clean his fingernails were?" my mother whispered when whoever it was had left, and I knew I was supposed to compare them to the fingernails of men who worked in the skin mills.

What I'd noticed, actually, was that none of the men on the island were missing fingers. As tanning and glove making became increasingly mechanized, there were more and more accidents, more men maimed. To make them less cumbersome and unwieldy, skins were halved, and cow hides in particular were too thick for gloves, which meant they had to be split. The staking machines used to stretch the skins, yielding more square footage, were particularly lethal, as were the embossing machines that used giant plates to give the leather a nice grain, and these descended with a force of a thousand pounds per square inch. And of course the clicker-cutter operators had to make sure their fingers were outside the perimeter of the machines when the skins were stamped. Every stage of the process now required machines and the hides were fed into these by hand, the very hand you'd lose if your mind wandered for an instant.

Blades sharp enough to sever a tanned skin were fitted with safety devices whose ostensible purpose was to keep them from lopping off fingers, but of course their real purpose was to protect the mill's owner from lawsuits. Because if you work the line, you're paid by the cubic foot of skin you process, and if you've got kids to feed and clothe, the very first thing you'll do is disable the safety mechanism that slows down your output. This is understood by everyone, including the foreman who turns his back while you do it. It's also understood that sooner or later something will go wrong. Work this mind-numbingly repetitive invites daydreaming, and your own safety often depends on people you're working with, because if you're pushing a skin into a machine, there's likely someone on the other side tugging it out. Eventually one of you will mess up. You'll slip or lunge and enter the machine with the same hand that people who summer on Martha's Vineyard shake with, after which your thumbnail will never be dirty again.

The Royal Society Beam House

Two years ago my daughter Kate was married in London at the Royal Society for the Arts, a series of underground vaults, formerly wine cellars, just off the Strand and a few short blocks from Trafalgar Square.

Our son-in-law, Tom, is English and the couple would be living in London, so there was no question of holding the ceremony in the States. The wedding was relatively small: Tom's family, some friends from the Slade Art School where they met, a few of Kate's college friends. Understandably, given the distance and expense, not many family members from our side of the Atlantic made the trip. The exception was my cousin Greg, with whom I shot wintry baskets when we were kids, and his wife, Carole, both of whom have lived their whole lives in Gloversville. "Quite a ways from Helwig Street," Greg said, taking in the venue. It wasn't as grand as "royal society" might suggest, but the arching brick vaults, candlelit for the occasion, were impressive. There's nothing remotely like it in an upstate mill town. The person who would've appreciated it the most, who'd have seen it as vindication for all those cheese sandwiches, was my mother, but she'd died that summer after a long illness.

In any event, the how-far-we'd-all-come theme occupied the American contingent while we waited for the bride and groom to finish having their photos taken. Nat Sobel, my friend and literary agent, immediately took to my cousin, telling Greg that as a boy he, too, had lived near a tannery that released its toxins into the local stream, the water running a different color each day depending on the dye batch. And so, flutes of prosecco in hand, we began swapping stories about the worst jobs we'd ever had.

I recalled the summer of my non-union construction job in Johnstown. Most other summers I'd been able to get union work at an hourly rate nearly twice what men were making at the skin mills. That meant joining the laborers' union, of course, and my father had to pay my dues while I was away at college. That year, though, jobs were scarce and I hadn't gotten one. Non-union construction was a different world. The first week we had to drill holes in a concrete abutment, not a difficult task if you have a drill. We didn't. What we did have was a jackhammer and a foreman who was unconstrained by conventional thinking. The jackhammer guy and I formed a team that afternoon. Balancing his weapon on my shoulder, I held on for dear life as we jacked horizontally into the wall, sharp shards of concrete blasting back into our faces. Another thing we didn't have was a spare set of goggles.

This story will win a lot of "bad job" storytelling contests unless your competitor has worked in the beam house of a skin mill doing the wettest, foulest, lowest paid, and most dangerous jobs in the whole tannery. Greg had worked in one a couple months one summer, and his younger brother, Jim, for much longer. The first and probably nastiest job in the beaming operation was unloading the skins, which arrived at the loading dock on railroad cars still reeking from the slaughterhouses. The word "skin" probably gives the wrong impression. Most people have never seen a hide — sheep, pig, calf, cow — unattached from its living owner. Stretched out flat they're big and, especially in the case of cows, surprisingly heavy. The top side is still covered with coarse hair, the underside with patches of maggot-infested flesh and gristle. The stench? You don't want to know, but imagine — if you can — what it must be like to spend an eight-hour shift unloading a railcar full of them in extreme temperatures.

Later, inside the beam house, things got even worse, the skins submerged in huge vats and soaked for days in a chemical bath that stripped off most of the hair and the last of the clinging flesh. Naturally, these chemicals could easily do the same to hair on the hands and forearms of men hired to hoist the soaked skins out of the vats, so they were issued long rubber gloves. You'd think the skins would be lighter minus the hair and flesh, but you'd be wrong, because untanned skins re-absorb the moisture lost during transport and this cleansing. The soaking also turns the heavy skins slippery. The rubber gloves make the slick skins harder to grab hold of, as does the fact that you're bent over the vat and standing on a wet concrete floor.

At some point, like the men farther down the line who prod the tanned skins into staking machines and roller presses, you'll do what you know you shouldn't. *You will take off the rubber gloves*, because then the job is immediately easier. At the end of your shift you will wash your hands and arms vigorously with the coarsest soap you can find, and when you get home you'll do it again. You'll gradually lose the hair on your hands and forearms, but otherwise, for awhile, everything seems fine. Okay, sometimes your fingers itch. A little at first, then a lot. Your skin begins to feel odd, almost loose, as if moisture has somehow gotten beneath it and what you're trying to scratch isn't on the surface. Finally it itches so bad you can't stand it anymore, and you grab your thumb or forefinger and give the skin a twist, then a pull. The skin, several layers of it, comes away in one piece, like the finger of a latex glove. (On the other side of the Atlantic, at the Royal Society for the Arts, my cousin demonstrates with his thumb, pulling off the imaginary prophylactic of skin, as everybody winces.) Instantly, the itching becomes stinging pain as the air impinges on your raw flesh. Later, someone will come around with a jar of black goop and you'll plunge your raw thumb into it, the coolness offering at least some relief, and for awhile you go back to wearing the rubber gloves.

This is only the beginning though, just the beam house's way of saying hello when all you want to say is goodbye — to the skins, the foul chemical air, even your coworkers, because let's face it, the ones who've been at it for a while, many of them with fifth grade educations, aren't quite right. You all make the same shitty pay, but at the end of the summer you get to leave and for that the others hate you. Meanwhile, you can't imagine getting used to work like this, nor that the day will ever come when the lunch whistle sounds and instead of going outside into the fresh air you'll decide it's easier to just stay where you are, take a seat on a pallet of decomposing hides, wipe your hands on your pants and eat your sandwich right there — because what the hell, it's been forever since you really smelled or tasted anything anyway. Plus, in the beam house there's entertainment. You can watch the rats chase the terrified cats that have been introduced to hunt them.

As my cousin relates this story, which I'm hearing for the first time, I become conscious of being in two places at once. I have one dry, wing-tipped foot in the candlelit world of a fancy arts society in London in 2007; the other work-booted foot is sloshing through the wet, slippery beam house floor in Gloversville, New York, circa 1970. That younger me isn't a novelist, or even a husband or father. He's just a twenty-year-old whose future can be stolen from him, who might indeed be complicit in the theft, because I remember all too well how sometimes, late in August, working road construction with my father, I'd think about not going back to college and maybe just staying on to do that hard, honest work he and his friends did all year round. The older me, now holding an empty champagne flute, feels guilty — and not, when I think of my home town, for the first time — to be where I am, like I've cheated destiny or, worse, swapped destinies with some other poor sod — to be where I am. My throat begins to constrict dangerously, though I can't tell if that's due to my cousin's story or because at this moment the wedding party returns — Kate absolutely radiant in the first hour of her marriage, and her sister Emily, who will marry the next year, laughing her throaty laugh and looping her arm through her fiancée's. Both smart, confident, beautiful young women, their feet planted squarely in the candlelit world before them, the only one that exists this day. The time may come when they, too, feel haunted, guilty about what they've been spared in life, keenly aware of how things, but for the grace of God, might have gone otherwise. But that day seems a long way off.

"More prosecco?" one of the waiters wants to know.

"Yes, please," I tell her. "Absolutely. Lay it on me. Right to the brim."

Civic Integrity

Not long after Kate's wedding, a package with a Gloversville return address arrived at our home in Maine. It contained two books. The first was a copy of *Bridge of Sighs*, which takes place in a fictional upstate New York town based on Gloversville, the story of two working-class boys, one who never leaves, the other who flees and never returns. The man who sent it in hopes of an autograph was Vincent DeSantis, who had spent most of his life in Gloversville, as he explained in the accompanying letter, and identified strongly with my character Lucy Lynch, who'd done the same thing. Clearly he thought he was writing to the boy who'd got away, and I couldn't really blame him. Since the death of my grandparents and my father, I've returned to Gloversville less and less frequently. The other book in his package was *Toward Civic Integrity: Re-establishing the Micropolis*, written by, well, Vincent DeSantis, and seeing this my heart sank, as it always does when I get sent books I haven't asked for with a view toward my endorsement. But Mr. DeSantis wasn't looking for a blurb, and his book, despite its rather scholarly title, wasn't an esoteric work of nonfiction. It was about Gloversville, and the question he posed was whether it and other small cities had a future in the global twenty-first century or were in inevitable and irreversible decline. "All is not lost in your home town," the author assured me. "A network of dedicated and talented individuals has lately been working to reassemble the pieces of this fractured micropolis." My knee-jerk reaction to this Humpty Dumpty sentiment was, *Yeah, right. All the king's horses and all the king's men.* Integrity indeed. I tossed the book on a tall stack of volumes whose common denominator was that I was unlikely to read them in this or any other lifetime. Not interested.

Yet that wasn't true, was it? After my mother's death, I'd been thinking a lot about her lifelong love-hate relationship with Gloversville. My cousin Greg had also been much on my mind. A few years earlier he'd had open heart surgery to replace a malfunctioning valve, but he still couldn't sleep lying down and was getting by on a couple hours a night. Since London, I'd tried to keep in touch, though when I called to inquire about his health, he always gave me his standard line, "Nah, I'm doing great for an old guy." Then we'd talk about what our kids were up to and what movies we'd seen and whether I was working on something new. But eventually the talk would turn to Gloversville: who'd been jailed or diagnosed, who'd gone into a nursing home or died. When I mentioned I couldn't get his beam house story out of my mind, he said, "Oh, hell, that's nothing," then launched into a litany of Gloversville woe I was all too familiar with. Men mangled by machines, men slowly poisoned, men killed in accidents. The three guys who worked the spray line in one mill all died of the same exotic testicular cancer, a case so outrageous it had made *The New York Times*. Not to mention the retarded boy hired to clean out the blues room, so named because the chrome used in these tanned skins turned them blue. The world of leather is full of scraps — strips of worthless skin and hoof and tail — and every now and then these had to be disposed of and the whole lethal place, including its giant vats, swamped out. One evening, when this kid didn't come home, his mother called the shop to see if he was still around. No, she was told, everybody from the day-shift had left. The following morning her son was found dead on the floor, asphyxiated by fumes. Another man, nearing retirement age, was working a press when his partner inadvertently stepped on the pedal that starts the rollers, catching the man's hand — more like a fin, now — in the mechanism. Another day, when it was weirdly cold on the floor, the foreman sent a man to fire up a boiler that hadn't been inspected in twenty years and it promptly blew up, killing him. Stories upon stories, each reminding my cousin of other men who died, their families uncompensated. Some dated back to my grandfather's days, stories I'd heard so many times that I know them as well as Greg does, but I understand why he needs to repeat them. The guys who lived this life in this world are, like World War II veterans, mostly gone. Somebody *should* give a shit.

For many months the vague boosterism of Vincent DeSantis's letter, together with my suspicion that his book was probably built on a shaky foundation of sentimentality and unguarded optimism, allowed me to let his book rest where I'd tossed it so contemptuously, until one day, suffering a rare attack of fair play (and perhaps just a bit curious), I picked it up and started reading. To my surprise I discovered that DeSantis and I had quite a lot in common, sharing many political and cultural convictions. It's clear to both of us, for instance, that the old manufacturing jobs that provided the economic life blood of towns like Gloversville are gone for good, no matter how much we might wish otherwise. We also agree that an America that makes less *is* less. He's as profoundly interested as I am in the New Urban movement and just as convinced that the time has come to start planning communities for people instead of their cars because the days of cheap energy are dwindling down to a precious few. A micropolis, as DeSantis defines it, is, like Gloversville, a small city of ten to fifty thousand inhabitants, and he argues persuasively that such communities might be well positioned to prosper in a less auto-centric future. They have the kind of infrastructure — a downtown — that will be essential, assuming urban renewal hadn't razed it back in the 60s. Ironically, abandoned mills, rather than being a blight on the landscape, could become part of the solution once they've been retrofitted to new purposes. Towns like Gloversville once had a rationale of their own, which is more than can be said for any suburb, and while their new incarnation is unlikely to have much in common with the old one, that doesn't mean it won't be just as valid. What Mr. DeSantis and I see eye-to-eye on, strangely enough, is the future, or at least a possible future.

But what a nest of thorns the past can be. "The glove industry sustained Gloversville in fine style," he enthuses. "Factories were full of glove cutters and glove makers, and the sound of sewing machines and the smell of finished leather…were a part of everyday life in Gloversville." I, too, happen to love the smell of finished leather, but I can love the smell only because I never worked in a beam house; and while I could be wrong, I'll hazard a wild guess that Mr. DeSantis never did either. But weren't there women in his family, as there were in mine, who sewed gloves for close to fifty years and when they finally retired earned pensions of less than fifty dollars a month? Mr. DeSantis's view of the Gloversville of our youth — it turns out he's just a year older than I — isn't false, but it rests on a foundation of carefully selected facts and memories. For him, the old days when the skin mills were in full swing were good because of the wealth and prosperity they generated. He remembers his aunts and uncles lamenting the loss of jobs overseas, but generously concludes that "in fairness to the glove companies… failure to take advantage…of cheap labor would have been tantamount to corporate suicide." Well, okay,

okay, but if a dramatic phrase like "corporate suicide" fairly describes the tanneries' untenable options in 1950, by the same token shouldn't disregard for the health and welfare of the workers who created their fortunes qualify as "corporate murder"? Or, coupled with a bottom line mentality that led so many to flee the scene of the crime, "corporate rape"? Chrome tanning was never anything but lethal, its byproducts including lime, chlorine, formaldehyde, sulfuric acid, chromium III, glycol ether EB, Toluene, xylol, magnesium sulfate, lead, copper, and zinc, to name just a few. Anyone who believes that tanneries didn't know they were releasing carcinogens into the air, water, and landfills probably also assumes that cigarette companies had no idea their product might be hazardous to the health of smokers. In addition to chasing cheap labor overseas, the big glove shops were fleeing — successfully for the most part — their own day of reckoning. New environmental restrictions imposed by the Department of Labor and later by the Occupational Safety and Health Administration were making the industry unprofitable, whereas on the other side of the world there were no such restrictions (and wouldn't be for decades). When it became clear that the tanneries wouldn't be allowed to continue dumping their waste in the stream, they left rather than pay the sewer taxes levied to support the new facility specifically designed and built to dispose of their waste more safely. Off they blithely went to pollute the Ganges and the Philippines, leaving behind a veritable Love Canal of carcinogens, the cleanup bill to be paid by the poisoned.

Of course Gloversville in its heyday, as Mr. DeSantis rightly points out, was more than glove shops and tanneries. A community, even one dominated by a single industry that hates competition, still needs grocery stores, bakeries, restaurants, insurance agencies, clothing stores, and car dealerships. Residents need schools and teachers and libraries and a movie theater, and when you lose the industry that underlies these other enterprises, they inevitably become endangered. It's not just the mills that are abandoned when the good times — if that's what they were — stop rolling. You also lose, as Mr. DeSantis points out, part of your identity, your reason for being, a shared sense of purpose that's hard to quantify. People who make things are often proud of what they make, especially if it endures. One summer my father and I worked on Exit 23 on the New York State Thruway, and thereafter were never able to get on that cloverleaf without sharing a knowing look. But sometimes people are so proud of what they make that they willingly overlook its true cost. That Gloversville once had an identity based on a common sense of purpose is a potent argument. It is used, for instance, to explain the construction of the great cathedrals of Europe, and what are they if not symbols of communal wealth and belief? Given the technology of the day, the pyramids are even more awe inspiring, at least until one remembers they were built with slave labor. Closer to home, the Confederacy was a case study in shared values and cultural identity, whose foundation, of course, was slavery; not long after the war that freed its victims, Margaret Mitchell invited the nation to lament the passing of those halcyon days that were now gone with the wind, and a great many still do.

Do I sound bitter?

High and Dry

A better question might be whether such bitterness can be justified. The optimism of Vincent DeSantis, in both his letter and his book, clearly struck a chord, and my reaction to it begs several questions. Among them: Is it possible I don't *want* Humpty Dumpty to be put back together again? Is Gloversville's current "shattered state" what I think, deep down, it somehow deserves? When I listen to my cousin's stories about men diagnosed, men maimed, men poisoned, men killed, isn't part of what I feel a grim satisfaction that so little in fact has changed? Morever, if it's bitterness I'm feeling toward my hometown, is it even my own, born of my own experience, or my mother's, a second-hand resentment I internalized as a kid and, as such, unrelated to stories of the beam house, the spray line, the tanning room. Perhaps most important, are all the old stories of injury and disease and death really just proxies, a chance for my cousin and me to vent rage that as boys we were too young to understand? After all, we witnessed the slow but fatal strangulation of our own grandfather, a man we both loved. Are we still, all these years later, bent on assigning blame?

Leather was a vertical industry. It went from low and wet in the beam house to high and dry in the sewing and cutting rooms, where the work was slightly better paying and less dangerous. I remember standing on the sidewalk below and sighting along my mother's index finger up to the top floor of the glove shop where my grandfather worked, and sensing her pride in him. I think I understood the verticality even then. But appearances were deceiving, and though he was as yet undiagnosed, my grandfather's luck had already run out. Machines and the relent-less drumbeat of piecework, together with a shorter work season, guaranteed that he'd die a poor man. And while the tanned skins were dry by the time they got to the top floor, they were also full of hide dust that, breathed over a lifetime, was toxic. For years my grandfather didn't worry about his shortness of breath. He'd come home from the Pacific with malaria, and maybe that explained it. In the early 60s, when it became impossible to ignore his worsening symptoms, he was finally diagnosed with emphysema by doctors who had little doubt that his occupation was a contributing factor. But he was also an occa-sional smoker, and never stopped, not entirely, even when he knew that each cigarette reduced the time he had left. I doubt he would've sued his employers even if he thought he could win because, as he would have been the first to point out, the glove shops had put bread on his family's table for all those years, and without them what would he have done, how would he otherwise have made a living? Bitterness and recrimination weren't worth the little breath he still had. In his way my grandfather was a philoso-pher, and he would've wanted me to be suspicious of any bitterness I harbored on his behalf, just as he would've reminded me of the terrible possibility that what nourishes us in this life may in some instances be the very thing that steals it from us.

When you take all this into account, it might be fair to ask why I, of all people, should continue to take his death and the betrayal of countless others so personally. After all, I never spent a minute in the beam house. Unlike my cousins, on hot summer days I don't have to lance with a needle the hard pustules that still form on their hands thirty years after the fact. What right does one who'd fled at the earliest opportunity have to speak for those who remained behind? I'm not, I like to think, an unforgiving man. Then why, when Vincent DeSantis informs me that all is not lost in my home town, does rage roil up uninvited out of the depths? Wouldn't it be better to make the peace my mother never made?

When the end drew near, she asked that her ashes be scattered not in Gloversville but on Martha's Vineyard, where she'd spent a week of her life. She knew that I vacationed there with my family every year. Maybe it wasn't her home, but home wasn't her home either. My cousin Greg, on the other hand, knows where home is. He has one and he lives there. When he tells me stories about men diagnosed, men maimed, men poisoned, men killed, it's his home he's talking about.

I'm often asked why I so seldom return to Gloversville, where I'm told people are proud of my success. I've written too many lies about the place, I like to explain, which is true enough. Reality chafes imagination and vice versa. And is there any need for me to return when, in a sense, I've never really left? Read my novels, even the ones not set in upstate New York, and you'll see Fulton County reflected on just about every page. It drove my mother crazy. She'd been hoping for a clean getaway, and mine was anything but. All too often my decisions in the present are linked to my Gloversville past. For instance. Because coastal Maine, where my wife and I live, is remote and I now have to travel a good deal, we recently got an apartment in downtown Boston with easy access to the airport and train station. We looked in a lot of different areas but finally settled, as I knew we would, in the Leather District, a neighborhood of mostly abandoned leather businesses. We're on the seventh floor of an eight-story building, high and dry, which I think would make my grandfather smile. One night shortly after we moved in, my wife was away and I found myself navigating through the unfamiliar television channels, stopping on one called American Life, which was playing an episode of *77 Sunset Strip*, which was followed by *Bourbon Street*

Beat and *Hawaiian Eye* and *Surfside 6*, all shows we watched when I was a boy stretched out on my grandparents' living room floor on Helwig Street. At some point I became aware of the tears streaming down my face, aware that I wasn't in Boston anymore, not really, but rather back in Gloversville, the only place I've ever called home and meant by that what people mean who never leave.

Richard Russo grew up in Gloversville, New York, and attended the University of Arizona, where he earned a Bachelor's degree, a Master of Fine Arts, and a PhD. He has taught at Southern Illinois University and Colby College, and is the author of seven novels, including *That Old Cape Magic*, *Bridge of Sighs*, and *Empire Falls*, which won the 2002 Pulitzer Prize. He has also written a collection of short stories and several produced screenplays. He lives in coastal Maine and Boston.

Kate Russo was born in Altoona, Pennsylvania, in 1982 and moved to Maine with her family at the age of nine. She has a Bachelor of Arts from Colby College and a Master of Fine Arts from The Slade School of Fine Art in London, England. She currently lives in Rockland, Maine, with her husband, the artist Tom Butler, whose knowledge of bookbinding and design were integral to the creation of this set. Her art has been exhibited all over England and recently at Susan Maasch Fine Art in Portland, Maine.